The Long
Red Scarf

Written by Nette Hilton

Illustrated by Margaret Power

Carolrhoda Books, Inc./Minneapolis

My grandfather likes to go fishing.

He fishes in the morning and in the evening.

He wears his old woolly cap with a pom-pom on it and his big blue sweater and his orange checked shirt.

Grandpa's friend Jake likes to go fishing too.
He fishes in the river and in the ocean.
He wears his old felt hat with the floppy brim and
his big green jacket and his yellow checked shirt and
a big, long, woolly, bright blue scarf.

Down by the river, late one night, the wind grew very, very cold.

How warm Jake looked in his big, long, woolly, bright blue scarf.

Grandpa admired the way Jake could wrap it around and around his neck and then tuck in the ends to keep his chest warm.

And he especially liked the way Jake could snuggle his chin into its warm blue folds.

My grandfather liked Jake's scarf so much he decided to ask Great Aunt Maude to knit him one that would be even longer and bigger and fuzzier…and the reddest red in the whole wide world.

So the very next day, while Great Aunt Maude was loading the truck with Bessie the cow and her two coffee-colored calves, Grandpa asked her.

"Maudie," he said, "Maudie, would you knit me a scarf that's the biggest, longest, fuzziest scarf in the reddest red in the whole wide world?"

Maudie paused. "Pop," she said (she calls my grandfather "Pop"), "I can drive the cows to their new green grassy paddock, and I can prime the pump to pump our water, and I can clean the fish you catch in the river, but I can't knit you the biggest, longest, fuzziest scarf in the reddest red in the whole wide world. I can't knit! Why don't you ask Cousin Isabel?"

Early the next morning, while Cousin Isabel was building a stand to hold her paint and brushes, my grandfather asked her.

"Izzy," he said, "Izzy, could you knit me a scarf that's the biggest, longest, fuzziest scarf in the reddest red in the whole wide world?"

Cousin Isabel balanced on the ladder. "Pop," she said (she calls my grandfather "Pop" too), "Pop, I can paint this room in clean bright colors all ready for my new baby, and I can build a cradle, and I can hang these curtains, but I can't knit you the biggest, longest, fuzziest scarf in the reddest red in the whole wide world. I don't have time!

"But I do have some wool of the reddest red and I do have some needles that go 'clicketty-click.' You could knit the biggest, longest, fuzziest scarf in the reddest red in the whole wide world yourself!"

"Humph!" said my grandfather.
"Humph!" And he stomped off to
get his fishing line.

It was very cold at the creek that night, and my grandfather grew colder and colder and more and more miserable.

His neck felt cold, his chest felt cold, even his ears felt cold.

"I bet I wouldn't be this cold if I had the biggest, longest, fuzziest scarf in the reddest red in the whole wide world," he mumbled miserably.

So the very next day, while Jake was washing his old fishing shirt, my grandfather asked him. "Jake," he said, "Jake, where did you get your big, long, woolly, bright blue scarf? I've asked Great Aunt Maude to knit me the biggest, longest, fuzziest scarf in the reddest red in the whole wide world, but she can't do it.

"I've asked Cousin Isabel to knit me the biggest, longest, fuzziest scarf in the reddest red in the whole wide world, but she *won't* do it. Jake, where did you get your big, long, woolly, bright blue scarf?"

"Stan," said Jake (my grandfather's name is Stan), "Stan, I knitted my big, long, woolly, bright blue scarf myself. I knitted it while I sat and waited for my dinner to cook. I knitted it when the sun went down and the world was still and quiet and all I could hear was the 'clicketty-click' of my needles."

Later that evening, while Cousin Isabel was busily building a cradle for her new baby, my grandfather asked her. "Izzy," he said, "Izzy, if I make you a hot cup of cocoa and some chocolate chip cookies, could you, would you find your wool of the reddest red and your needles that go 'clicketty-click' so I can make the biggest, longest, fuzziest, scarf in the whole wide world myself?"

My grandfather still likes to go fishing.
So does his friend Jake.

But now, if you listen carefully when the sun is going down and the world is still and quiet, you might hear "clicketty-click, clicketty-clack" as my grandfather and his friend Jake sit
together
and
knit . . .

…a tiny yellow hat in the softest, fluffiest wool, a small nubby jacket in the snowiest, whitest wool, and a little fuzzy scarf in the reddest red in the whole wide world, just in case it's chilly when new baby Susan comes fishing with them.

Author's Dedication: To Stan

Illustrator's Dedication: To my father
who fished, and to my mother
who filleted the catch—*and knitted*

This edition first published in the U.S. in 1990 by Carolrhoda
Books, Inc.

Text copyright © 1987 by Nette Hilton
Illustrations copyright © 1987 by Margaret Power
First published 1987 by Omnibus Books, Adelaide, Australia in
association with Penguin Books Australia Ltd.

LIBRARY OF CONGRESS CATALOGING-IN-PUBLICATION DATA

Hilton, Nette.
    The long red scarf / by Nette Hilton ; illustrations by Margaret
Power.
      p.   cm.
    "First published 1987 by Omnibus Books, Adelaide, Australia in
association with Penguin Books Australia Ltd."—T.p. verso.
    Summary: After all his female relatives refuse to knit him a scarf
as they go on about their business—driving the cows, building a
crib—Grandfather learns to knit himself.
      ISBN 0-87614-399-0 (lib. bdg.)
      [1. Sex role—Fiction. 2. Scarves—Fiction.] I. Power,
Margaret, ill. II. Title.
PZ7.H56775Lo   1990
[E]—dc20
                                          89-35729
                                             CIP
                                             AC
Manufactured in the United States of America

2 3 4 5 6 7 8 9 10 99 98 97 96 95 94 93 92 91

6/92